Press Play

Also by Anne Fine

How to Write Really Badly
The Country Pancake
The Angel of Nitshill Road
Bill's New Frock
Anneli the Art Hater
Scaredy Cat
Countdown
Design-a-Pram
A Sudden Puff of Glittering Smoke
A Sudden Swirl of Icy Wind
A Sudden Glow of Gold

Telling Tales – An Interview with Anne Fine

For older readers
The Summer House Loon
The Other Darker Ned
The Granny Project
The Stone Menagerie
Very Different

Anne Fine
Children's Laureate

Press
Play

EGMONT

First published in Great Britain 1994
by Piccadilly Press Ltd
This edition reissued 2002
by Egmont Books Limited,
239 Kensington High Street, London W8 6SA

Text copyright © Anne Fine 1994
Illustration copyright © Jim Kavanagh 1996
Cover illustration copyright © Lee Gibbons 2002

The moral rights of the author, illustrator
and cover illustrator have been asserted.

ISBN 1 4052 0185 1

A CIP catalogue record for this title
is available from the British Library

Typeset by Dorchester Typesetting Group Ltd
Printed and bound by
Cox & Wyman, Reading, Berkshire

Contents

Chapter 1   *1*

Chapter 2   *9*

Chapter 3   *14*

Chapter 4   *24*

Chapter 5   *30*

Chapter One

When the alarm went off, Nicky and Tasha sat up in their beds and stared. Mum wasn't there, but the cassette-player was on the floor by Little Joe's cot. On top of it was a note.

'*Press Play*,' said the note.

That was all.

'Go on, then,' said Tasha. 'Press Play.'

So Nicky slid out of bed and pressed Play. They both watched as the tape inside started to go round and round, and out came their mother's cheerful early morning voice.

'*Wakey-wakey!*'

'Creepy!' said Nicky, and Little Joe gripped
his cot bars and pushed out his bottom lip,
ready to cry, as the voice went on.

'*I had to go in to work really early today. And
your dad had to work all night, so he's still
sleeping.*'

'We'll have to sort ourselves out, then,'
muttered Tasha.

2

'*You'll have to sort yourselves out,*' Mum's voice echoed through the room.

Little Joe burst into tears. They spurted out so hard they missed his face completely, and fell on the carpet.

'*You'd better do Little Joe first,*' their mother's voice floated out. '*He might be a bit upset, hearing my voice, but me not being there.*'

3

'Too right,' said Nicky, and he went across to haul Little Joe over the bars of the cot.

As soon as he felt safe in his brother's arms, Little Joe stopped crying and started to poke his fingers in Nicky's ears. Nicky dumped him down on the potty.

'I'll dress him,' he said to Tasha, 'if you'll feed him.'

'No, no, no, no, no, no,' said Tasha. 'He

spat porridge all down me yesterday. I'll dress him. You feed him.'

'We'll toss for it,' said Nicky.

He was just breaking into Tasha's money box for a coin when their mother's voice started up again.

'*Nicky, you change him. And Tasha, you feed him.*'

'Thanks, Mum,' groaned Tasha. 'Thanks a bunch!'

'*Now,*' said the voice. '*While Nicky's sorting out Little Joe, Tasha can get dressed, and carry me down carefully into the kitchen.*'

'What?' Tasha said. 'What is she on about?'

Nicky took Little Joe's hand and tugged him over to a pile of fresh clothes beside the cot.

'She means the cassette-player,' said Nicky. 'She means you have to carry it downstairs.'

'Why?'

'I don't know,' Nicky said. 'So she can keep bossing us about, I suppose.'

'Hmph!' said Tasha, who was always a little bit grumpy in the mornings.

Draping her clean clothes over the cassette-player, she picked it up and carried it, very carefully, as far as the top of the stairs. Then she put it down safely and went into the bathroom with her clothes.

Press Play

She was just drying her face when, outside the door, she heard a strange whispering.

'What is it?' she called.

Nobody answered, but the whispering carried on.

'Is that you, Nicky?' Tasha shouted. 'What do you *want?*'

He didn't answer, but the whispering kept up.

'Say it louder!' yelled Tasha. 'I can't *hear* you!'

She stopped to listen. The whispering was still going on outside the door.

'Speak *up!*' bellowed Tasha. 'Speak up! Speak up! Speak *up!*'

She flung the door open, and rushed out.

The tape was still going. And so was her mother's voice, in a whisper.

'. . . *so remember what I say, you're not to wake Daddy up unless you really need him, so that means you've got to keep very, very quiet all the time you're in the bathroom . . .*'

'Oh, gggrrrr!' growled Tasha.

But she growled it quietly.

Chapter Two

Little Joe sat in the highchair and banged his fist on the tray.

'Don't forget to strap him in properly,' Tasha said, guessing the next bit on the tape.

'*Don't forget to strap Joe in properly,*' came from the tape. '*I've made his porridge. All you have to do is heat it up.*'

Stirring the porridge, Tasha opened and closed her mouth like an actor on telly with the sound turned down while her mother's voice poured off the tape.

'*I hope you've chosen something sensible to wear,*

9

Tasha. It looks pretty chilly out there. I hope you're not wearing something silly like that thin cotton cowboy shirt.'

Tasha looked down at her thin cotton cowboy shirt.

'You should be wearing something nice and warm, like that pretty red woolly Granny knitted for you.'

Tasha leaned over the pan full of Little Joe's porridge and pretended to throw up in it.

Little Joe's eyes widened. Then he stuck out his bottom lip, ready to cry again.

'It's all right,' Tasha told him. 'I didn't do anything. I was only joking. Here it comes now. Lovely porridge!'

She put the bowl on his tray, and handed him the spoon.

'Don't want it!' said Little Joe.

'Course you do,' said Tasha.

'Don't!'

'Do!'

'He doesn't want it because he thinks you threw up in it,'

said Nicky.

Tasha turned to Little Joe.

'Look,' she said to him. 'Watch.'

Leaning over the bowl, she pretended to throw up in it all over again.

'See?' she told him. 'Jokey-jokey! There's nothing wrong with the porridge.'

Little Joe banged his spoon on the tray.

'Jokey-jokey!' he shouted. 'Jokey-jokey!'

'He wants you to do it again,' said Nicky.

'Well, he's out of luck,' said Tasha.

Just at that moment, out of the cassette-player their mother's voice floated across the room.

'I hope you're making sure Little Joe's eating his breakfast.'

Sighing, Tasha did it

11

again. Little Joe
laughed so
hard, his
cheeks
wobbled.

'Again!'
he told Tasha.

'No,' Tasha said. 'Eat your porridge.'

'Again!'

'No!'

'Again!'

Little Joe banged his spoon hard in the
bowl. A great lump of porridge flew out and
landed on Tasha's thin cotton cowboy shirt.

'Thank you,' said Tasha. 'Thank you very
much.'

Press Play

Still dripping porridge, she slid off her seat and made for the door.

'*If you're nice to him, he shouldn't give you any trouble at all,*' the voice from the cassette assured her as she slowly climbed the stairs.

Back in the bedroom, Tasha rooted through her cupboard, looking for something else to wear. There wasn't much. Half her clothes were in the mending pile. The other half were in the wash. In the end, just as she feared, Tasha could only find one thing.

Sighing, she pulled it over her head.

It was the pretty red woolly Granny knitted for her.

Chapter Three

Nicky stood listening to the list of things he had to get ready for Little Joe.

'*He'll need his big plastic Snoopy lunchbox,*' Mum was saying on the tape. '*And his juice bottle. And his spare pair of underpants. And his dummy. And, of course, Rabbit.*'

Little Joe bounced up and down in his highchair.

'Wabbit!' he shouted. 'Wabbit! Wabbit! Wabbit!'

'Just a minute,' said Nicky. 'I have to find the other things as well. They're just as important as Rabbit.'

'Wabbit!' Little Joe pounded his fists on the tray in front of him. 'Wabbit! Wabbit! Wabbit!'

Nicky looked round. There, at the end of the table, was the big plastic Snoopy lunchbox.

'Right,' he said. 'That's one. Only four to go.'

He kept looking. The juice bottle was nowhere to found.

Nor were the spare pair of underpants or the dummy.

'I can't even see Rabbit,' muttered Nicky.

Press Play

'Wabbit!' screamed Little Joe. 'Wabbit! Wabbit! Wabbit!'

Anne Fine

'Just be quiet,' Nicky told Little Joe sternly, unstrapping him and lifting him out of the highchair. 'Just yelling doesn't help. If you want to be useful, go round the house and *look* for things. Don't just stand there yelling Rabbit.'

Press "Play"

'Wabbit!' screeched Little Joe. 'Wabbit! Wabbit! Wabbit!'

Nicky shoved his face close to Little Joe's.

'Shut up!' he yelled back. 'Shut up! Shut up! Shut up!'

'Wabbit! yelled Little Joe. 'Wabbit! Wabbit! Wabbit!'

Anne Fine

Losing his temper, Nicky snatched a tea towel off the rack, and hurled it at Little Joe's head.

Furious, Little Joe snatched the big plastic Snoopy lunchbox off the table, and hurled it at Nicky.

Nicky jumped out of the way, fast.

The lunchbox landed with a crash on the

floor. The clasps flew open. Out fell the juice bottle, the spare pair of underpants, the dummy and Rabbit.

'Wabbit!' shrieked Little Joe with glee.

Anne Fine

'Wabbit! Wabbit! Wabbit!'

He ran across and scooped Rabbit up in his arms. Then he sat on the floor in the corner and cuddled her, twisting one of her long velvet ears around his finger while Nicky filled the juice bottle, took the sandwich marked 'Joe – Thursday' out of the freezer, and packed him a banana and a nut bar. He was just rinsing the dummy under the tap when Tasha came down again.

'Everything going OK?' she asked him.

'Fine,' Nicky said. 'No problem.'

Their mother's voice came from the tape.

Press Play

'*Right,*' it was saying. '*Quite sure you've got everything for Joe?*'

'Quite sure, thanks,' Nicky told the tape grimly.

But the voice was checking them over one more time, just to be safe:

'*Big plastic Snoopy lunchbox, juice bottle, spare pair of underpants, dummy and Rabbit?*'

'Wabbit!' said Little Joe ecstatically, wrapping her ears tightly around her and squeezing hard. 'Wabbit! Wabbit! Wabbit!'

Chapter Four

'*Now,*' said their mother's voice. '*If you're quite sure you've had enough breakfast and you're all packed for school, it's time to reset the alarm clock for one o'clock, and put it next to Daddy's bed –*'

'Without *waking* him?' demanded Tasha.

'*– without waking him,*' the tape said.

'Serious stuff,' said Tasha, eyeing Little Joe suspiciously.

'We'll need a plan,' agreed Nicky.

First, they tried Plan A. Tasha sat Little Joe on her knee and sang him nursery rhymes, very softly, while Nicky fetched the alarm and

Press Play

reset it, then crept along the landing towards the big bedroom.

Little Joe tried poking Tasha to make her sing louder. When it didn't work, he wriggled out of her lap and rushed off to fetch Nicky.

Tasha rushed after him.

Next, they tried Plan B. Tasha sneaked away with the alarm clock and Nicky sat Little Joe on the draining board and told him the story of the Three Bears while he was washing up. But Little Joe got excited when he heard the word porridge, and banged his heels on the cupboard doors.

Nicky lifted him down, and he broke away and ran after Tasha.

In the end, they used Plan C. Tasha explained to Little Joe that it was a game, and he had to be quiet.

'Sssh!' she said, putting a finger on her lips.

'Sssh!' said Little Joe, copying her.

Anne Fine

'Quieter than that,' warned Tasha.

'Ssssssh!'

'Ssssssh!' said Little Joe, very, very quietly. Together they went up the stairs. Nicky pushed open the door to the big bedroom.

'Ssssssh!' Little Joe said, but he said it quietly.

Daddy lay on his back on his side of the big bed. One arm was flung out, and his head was

back. There was nasty black stubble all over his cheeks and his chin, and he was snoring loudly.

'Ssssh!' Little Joe told him sternly. 'Ssssh!'

Nicky crept to the side of the bed and put down the alarm clock reset for one o'clock. Little Joe followed Nicky, and Tasha followed Joe, in case he suddenly started fussing.

'Sssssh!' Joe warned everyone.

The three of them stood in a line beside the bed and looked down at their stubbly, snoring father. Whenever he reached the main part of each breath, his whole jaw shuddered and a flap of sheet under his nose flew up in the air. There was oil on his forehead and oil under his fingernails, and his pyjamas were not buttoned up.

'Yuk,' Little Joe said. 'Yuk.'

'Too right,' said Tasha. 'If this is what he looks like in the morning, good thing it's Mum who kisses us goodbye.'

Just then their father snorted in his sleep, smacking his lips like a chimpanzee, and letting his mouth fall wide open.

'Kiss Daddy goodbye,' Nicky teased Joe.

Joe stuck out his bottom lip.

Hastily, Tasha took his hand and pulled him towards the door.

'Let's just *blow* Daddy a kiss,' she said. 'He'll like that. So will you.'

Joe's lip went in again.

'Smart thinking, Tash,' said Nicky.

The three of them stood in a line by the door, and, one by one, blew a kiss to their sleeping father.

Then they left, shutting the door very quietly behind them.

Chapter Five

As soon as Little Joe had gone off to playgroup with Flora and Mrs Bundy from next door, Nicky and Tasha raced around the house, following orders from the tape.

Press Play

'Have you turned off the taps in the bathroom properly? Especially the hot tap?'

Nicky raced upstairs to check on the hot tap.

'Is the cat out?'

Tash chased the cat out.

'And don't forget to lock the back door.'

Tasha locked the back door.

'Is the oven off?'

Nicky checked it.

'And the grill! Don't forget the grill!'

Nick checked the grill – twice.

Anne Fine

'*Is the fridge door shut?*'
'Yes,' Tasha told the tape. 'Yes, it's shut.'

'*Have you switched your bedroom light off?*'
Now it was Tasha's turn to race upstairs.

'*And put the empty milk bottles out on the step?*'
Nicky did that, while Tasha raced downstairs again.

'*And have you found your jackets and your school bags?*'
'Yes, yes, yes.'

32

Press Play

'*And taken your lunch money off the shelf?*'

Nicky passed one pile of coins to Tasha, and dropped the others in his pocket.

'Yes, yes, yes.'

'*What else?*' the voice on the tape said, stopping for a think.

'Have you fed the elephant?' muttered Tasha.

'And switched on the rocketship parked on the roof?' added Nicky.

'And locked Mad Old Aunt Lucy in the coal cellar?'

Anne Fine

'With her rat poison sandwiches?'

'*I can't think of anything else,*' said the voice on the tape. '*I hope there's nothing I've forgotten.*

'Nicky's sub-machine gun?' suggested Tasha.

'Tasha's diamonds?'

'Nicky's pet armadillo?'

'Tasha's dirt-bike?'

'*Of course!*' the tape said. '*Your homework reading books! They're stuck in the toast rack.*'

Nicky rushed over to fetch them.

Press Play

'*That's it, then,*' said the tape. '*I think you're probably ready to go. Now, without waking Daddy, put on your jackets, pick up your school bags and tiptoe to the front door. Drop the catch on the lock, and pull the door closed behind you.*'

'Very quietly,' prompted Tasha.

'*Very quietly,*' said the tape.

Together, they pulled on their jackets and picked up their school bags. They didn't wait for the voice on the tape. They started chanting the next bit all by themselves.

Anne Fine

'*And be good, and be careful, and stick together till you get to the main road, and make sure you cross with the lollipop lady.*'

Nicky and Tasha had finished chanting the daily speech well before the voice on the tape limped to the end.

Then they tiptoed away from the cassette-player towards the front door.

'*Goodbye, darlings,*' the voice on the tape called after them.

'Goodbye,' called Nicky and Tasha.

They let the catch down, and pulled the door shut and locked behind them. Then they turned to one another, and said:

'Phew!'

Anne Fine

Back in the kitchen, there was a silence as the tape ran on towards its end. Then, suddenly, the voice said:

'*Phew*!'

And it fell silent.

BiLL'S NEW FROCK

Bill Simpson wakes up to find he's a girl, and, worse, his mother makes him wear a frilly pink dress to school. How on earth is he going to survive a whole day like this?

Everything just seems to be *different* for girls . . .

'Stylishly written and thought-provoking' *Guardian*

'. . . a gem. Don't miss it.' *TES*

WINNER OF THE SMARTIES PRIZE

HOW TO WRITE rEallY BAdLY

Chester Howard can see Joe's project 'How to Write Neatly' can only be a disaster. Bottom of the class, Joe makes a terrible mess of his work, jumbling letters and numbers up together.

But a project called 'How to Write Really Badly' – now there's something Joe can do better than anyone else.

And Chester is about to find there's a lot more to Joe than he expected . . .

'Screamingly funny' *The Herald*

'Fine has a rare genius for building a funny, enriching and moving story around the nuts and bolts of school life' *The Times*

WINNER OF THE *TES* NASEN AWARD

The Country Pancake

Lancelot's lovely teacher, Miss Mirabelle, is in big trouble.

She's told a giant whopper and unless she can come up with a brilliant plan, she's going to look very, *very* silly.

Can Lancelot help this damsel in distress?

'this entirely charming tale of an unconventional teacher, a suspicious head, an imaginative class and a co-operative cow.' *TES*